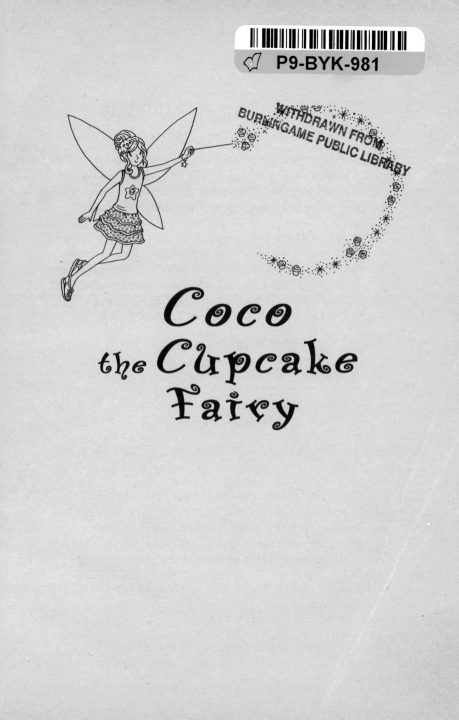

Coco the Cupcake Fairy

Special thanks to Rachel Elliott

ISBN 978-0-545-60533-5

Previously published as Sweet Fairies #3: *Coco the Cupcake Fairy* by Orchard U.K. in 2013.

All rights reserved. Published by Scholastic Inc., 557 Broadway, New York, NY 10012, by arrangement with Rainbow Magic Limited.

12 11 10 9 8 7 6 5 4 3 2 1   14 15 16 17 18 19/0

Printed in the U.S.A.   40

This edition first printing, March 2014

Coco the Cupcake Fairy

by Daisy Meadows

SCHOLASTIC INC.

The Fairyland Palace

Candy Land

Goblins' ice cream truck

Market booths

Charlie's ice cream truck

Kirsty's House

Wetherbury Village

Jack Frost's
Ice Castle

Fair

The Park

Candy
Shop

High St.

I have a plan to make a mess
And cause the fairies much distress.
I'm going to take their charms away
And make my dreams come true today!

I'll build a castle made of sweets,
And ruin the fairies' silly treats.
I just don't care how much they whine,
Their cakes and candies will be mine!

Contents

A Sweet Surprise

"This has been such an exciting day," said Rachel Walker, licking her Marshmallow Magic ice cream. "We've already been to Fairyland *and* helped two fairies get their magic charms back from Jack Frost."

Rachel and her best friend, Kirsty Tate, were walking home from the Wetherbury village square, where they had been looking around the market.

Rachel was visiting Kirsty for spring break, and it looked like they were going to have an exciting week.

"The day's not over yet," added Kirsty, smiling. She paused to lick her Strawberry Sparkle ice cream, which was melting in the hazy afternoon sun and running over her fingers. "I have a feeling that now that magical things have *started* happening, they're going to *keep* happening!" she went on, licking her fingers one by one.

No one in the human world knew that the girls had been on many adventures in

Fairyland. They were always excited to make new fairy friends and help outwit Jack Frost and his naughty goblins. That morning, Honey the Candy Fairy had visited them to ask for help again. This time, Jack Frost and his goblins had stolen the seven magic charms belonging to the Sugar and Spice Fairies. Without them, all of the candy and treats in both the human world and Fairyland were ruined!

"We've already rescued Lisa the Lollipop Fairy's magic lollipop charm and Esme the Ice Cream Fairy's magic ice cream cone charm," Rachel said, chewing on a deliciously sticky marshmallow. "But there are still five more charms to find."

"And if we don't find them fast,

Fairyland's Treat Day will be ruined!" said Kirsty, biting her lip.

The day after tomorrow was Treat Day in Fairyland. King Oberon and Queen Titania always gave a basket of special treats to each fairy to thank them for their hard work all year. But Jack Frost was using the Sugar and Spice Fairies' magic charms to get all the treats for himself. There weren't any left for the fairies! He was planning to build a giant Candy Castle, and he had given the magic charms to his goblins for safekeeping.

The goblins had come to the human world to find even *more* treats to steal for the Candy Castle. Rachel and Kirsty kept a careful lookout for the little green troublemakers as they walked past the village hall. They knew that goblins could pop up anywhere!

"It's not just magical things that we have to look forward to," Rachel reminded her friend. "It's almost your birthday, and Aunt Helen said that she left a surprise waiting for you at home, remember?"

Aunt Helen had visited earlier that day for lunch, but then she had to go back to work. She had an important job at Candy Land, the big treat factory on the hill overlooking Wetherbury.

"*Ooh*, you're right!" said Kirsty,

crunching on the last piece of her cone. "Come on, let's run the rest of the way!"

The girls ran up Kirsty's street and burst through her front door, panting and giggling.

"Hello, girls!" said Mrs. Tate, peeking out of the kitchen and smiling at them. "Did you have a good time?"

"Magical!" said Rachel, thinking of all their adventures so far.

"Kirsty, there's something waiting for you on the dining room table," said Mrs. Tate.

The girls exchanged excited smiles, then kicked off their shoes and hurried through to the dining room. There, they found an envelope propped up against the fruit bowl. It was pink, and Kirsty's name was written in swirly gold letters on the front.

Eagerly, Kirsty opened the envelope and pulled out two pink cards with sparkly edges. She gasped as she read the words on the cards.

"These are tickets for a tour of Candy

Land," she told Rachel. "Look—there's one for you, too!"

"And the tour is tomorrow!" said Rachel. "What a fantastic present!"

"I just hope that we can stop Jack Frost from ruining all the treats at Candy Land—and everywhere else," said Kirsty, her face falling slightly. "If we can't help the rest of the Sugar and Spice

Fairies find their magic charms, our tour
will be a disaster!"

Rachel frowned. Kirsty was right.
They had to find those missing
charms—and they didn't have much
time!

Baking Blunders

As the girls gazed at the Candy Land tickets, Mrs. Tate came over and put her arms around their shoulders.

"Girls, would you like to bake some cupcakes?" she asked.

"*Ooh*, yes, please!" said Kirsty.

"We could give some to your aunt Helen to thank her for the tickets," Rachel suggested.

"That's a great idea," said Kirsty. "I want to make our cupcakes as pretty as the ones at Cupcake Corner."

"Is that the new shop in the village?" asked Mrs. Tate, as she started gathering the ingredients. "They always have delicious-  looking cakes in the window."

"Ours are going to be just as yummy," said Rachel with a grin.

"You can make the cupcake batter on your own," said Mrs. Tate. "Call me when you're ready, and I'll help put the cupcakes in the oven."

She left the kitchen and closed the door behind her. Kirsty looked at the recipe book.

"I'll measure out the flour and sugar while you beat the eggs," she suggested.

Rachel nodded eagerly, but as she picked up the carton of eggs, it slipped out of her hand. SMASH! Six eggs lay broken on the kitchen floor, oozing across the tiles.

"Oh, no." Rachel groaned. "What a mess!"

"Don't worry," said Kirsty. "We have another carton of eggs in the fridge."

While Kirsty measured out the flour, Rachel cleaned up the mess and got out  the other carton of eggs. As she was beating them, Kirsty gave a squeal—and a huge puff of white flour covered both girls. "Sorry!" Kirsty exclaimed. "I lost my grip on the bag and dumped too much flour into the bowl."

"We're not doing very well, are we?" Rachel laughed, blinking flour out of her eyes and shaking it from her hair. "It's

OK, we can just tip it back into the bag."

Soon, the cupcake batter was ready.

"Let's take turns stirring it," said
Kirsty. "The recipe says to 'stir quickly.'"

She plunged a wooden spoon into the
bowl and stirred hard. Globs of cupcake
batter flew
everywhere!

"Careful!"
cried Rachel.
"Here, let
me try."

But as
soon as
she moved the
spoon, batter splattered into the waiting
cupcake wrappers.

"Hey!" squealed a tiny, bell-like voice.

"That came from *inside* one of the
cupcake wrappers," said Rachel in
astonishment. "Oh, Kirsty, look! That
one is glowing!"

As the girls leaned in closer, Coco the
Cupcake Fairy peeked out of the yellow
cupcake wrapper,
a dollop of cake
batter on the
tip of her nose.

"Hello, girls,"
she said with
a giggle. "I
wasn't expecting that!"

"Sorry, Coco!" Rachel exclaimed.
"We've been trying to make cupcakes,
but everything seems to be going all
wrong."

"No problem," said Coco with a smile, wiping the cupcake batter off the tip of her nose. "Cupcakes are my favorite things—even before they're cooked! I just wish that I had my magic cupcake charm so I could help make your cupcakes perfect. I'm here to ask if you'll help me get it back from Jack Frost and his goblins."

"Of course we will!" Kirsty replied. "We'll start looking as soon as we're done baking."

Just then, Mrs. Tate came back into the kitchen. Coco zoomed into Rachel's pocket as quick as a flash!

"Are the cupcakes ready to go in the oven?" asked Mrs. Tate.

"Almost," said Rachel, spooning the batter into the cupcake wrappers.

Kirsty helped her fill all the wrappers, and then Mrs. Tate used her oven mitts to put the tray into the oven.

"Let's make some colorful icing while the cupcakes are baking," suggested Mrs. Tate.

Rachel decided to make some purple icing, and Kirsty chose pink. But as soon as Rachel started to stir her mixture, she groaned.

"I must have done something wrong," she said. "My icing looks gray!"

"Nothing's going right!" exclaimed Kirsty.

She hurried over to look in Rachel's bowl, but her foot slipped on a glob of icing that had fallen on the floor.

"WHOOPS!" She squealed as she skidded across the kitchen.

Rachel held out her arms. Kirsty clutched them and stopped herself from falling. Her heart was thudding!

"Thank you, Rachel!" she panted.

Just then, the oven timer rang.

"*Ooh*, the cupcakes are ready!" said

Rachel. "We can just use plain white icing to frost them."

Mrs. Tate put on her oven mitts and opened the oven door. A bit of black smoke puffed out as she peered inside.

"Oh, no!" she exclaimed.

She pulled out the tray of cupcakes and the girls looked at them in dismay. Some were burned, while others didn't seem to have cooked at all. A couple had spilled out of their wrappers. They were all ruined!

Fairy Spies

"Girls, I think you must have made a mistake with the recipe," said Mrs. Tate, coughing as more black smoke billowed out of the oven.

"What a disaster," Kirsty said, sounding miserable. "I tried to follow the recipe so carefully, but these look nothing like the cupcakes at Cupcake Corner."

While Mrs. Tate scraped the burned batter off the cupcake tray, Rachel pulled Kirsty aside. Her eyes were sparkling with sudden excitement.

"Kirsty, I bet Jack Frost's greedy goblins are at Cupcake Corner," she whispered. "I think they must have Coco's magic charm, and that's why the cupcakes in the shop are so perfect."

Kirsty's eyes opened wide. "You're

right!" she said. "But how are we going to stop them?"

"I have an idea," said Rachel, turning to Kirsty's mom. "Mrs. Tate, could we go to Cupcake Corner to buy some cupcakes for later, since ours turned out so awful?"

"I think that's a very good idea," said Mrs. Tate.

Rachel and Kirsty changed their shoes and picked up their purses. Then they hurried outside, with Coco still safely tucked in Rachel's pocket.

The girls ran all the way to Cupcake
Corner, hoping that they were right
about the goblins. They stopped in front
of the window to catch their breath,
gazing at the display of beautifully iced
cupcakes.

"They're so
pretty," said
Coco, popping
her head out of
Rachel's pocket.
"Look at the red
ones. They're
arranged to look like
a bunch of roses!"

"I like the butterfly shape," said Kirsty,
pointing to a large pink-and-white
display in the middle of the window.

"They all look delicious," said Rachel, gazing at a tall stand holding tiers of iced cupcakes. Each one was decorated with a tiny candy fairy. "My stomach's growling!"

"I wonder why Jack Frost wants *these* cupcakes to be perfect," said Kirsty. "I'm

sure the baker is selling plenty of them!"

"Look," said Rachel, peering past the displays into the shop. "There's a man with lots of kids at the counter. I wonder if he's buying some cupcakes for a party."

Just then, the shortest kid turned

around and made
a face at the girls.
They both
gasped. The
face was green!

"Those kids are
goblins!" Kirsty
exclaimed.

"And that man is wearing an ice-blue
cape," added Rachel with a shiver. "I bet
it's Jack Frost. We have to find out what
he's up to!"

"Coco, will you turn us into fairies?"
asked Kirsty. "Then we can stay out of
sight and hear what they're saying."

"Good idea!" said Coco, fluttering out
of Rachel's pocket.

Luckily, there was no one else on the
street. The girls ducked down below the

window ledge so that the goblins couldn't see them.

Coco balanced on Kirsty's knee, standing on one foot like a ballerina. Her golden-brown hair gleamed, and the jewels in her hair sparkled in the afternoon sun. She waved her wand in a wide circle until hundreds of tiny, sparkling cupcakes flew from it. They whirled around Rachel and Kirsty, who suddenly smelled the delicious aroma of baking cake!

Their skin tingled as the magic began

to work, and they shrank to fairy-size.
Pastel wings appeared on their backs and
they fluttered them in excitement,
twirling up into the air.

"Come on, let's go inside," said Rachel,
leading the way into the shop through a
small open window. They hid behind
some cupcakes on the top tier of a cake
stand, peeking out carefully.

Jack Frost was standing at the counter
in his ice-blue cape, talking to the baker.

Three goblins
were next to
him, all
wearing
green shorts
and T-shirts
with cupcakes
on the front.
While Jack Frost was talking, they were
sneaking nibbles of the cupcakes on
display around the shop.

"Look!" Coco whispered. "Even their
hats are shaped like cupcakes."

"What is Jack Frost saying?" asked
Kirsty. "We have to find out!"

A Rude Customer

"And don't forget to draw my face on each cupcake in blue icing," the girls heard Jack Frost snap. "There had better not be a single cupcake without my face on it! Do you hear me?"

"Yes, sir," said the baker, looking surprised at Jack Frost's rudeness. "But I'll need a picture to copy."

"That's easy," said Jack Frost, pulling a photo out of his pocket. "I always carry a few pictures of myself around with me. I like to have something handsome to look at sometimes, instead of this ugly bunch."

He jerked his thumb at the goblins, and the baker gave a nervous laugh.

"He thinks Jack Frost is joking," Kirsty whispered with a little grin.

"Are you having a party, sir?" asked the baker, writing down the order.

"Party?" Jack Frost exclaimed. "No!

I'm going to use lots and lots of cupcakes to make myself a throne, of course. Look, here's my design."

He thrust a crumpled piece of paper under the baker's nose.

"But . . . but . . . if you try to sit on the cupcakes, you'll squish them," said the baker.

"Are you calling me FAT?" roared Jack Frost.

"No, sir!" the baker cried, shaking

his head. He changed the subject. "Now, this is a very big order, so it will take us some time. Maybe you'd like to come back later?"

"We'll wait," Jack Frost growled.

The baker looked alarmed and hurried into the kitchen.

"That silly baker doesn't know my clever plan," said Jack Frost, rubbing his bony hands together. "When the cupcakes are finished, I'll add an ingredient of my own—a magic spell that will make them strong enough to sit on. Then I can finally relax on a cushion of soft, tasty cake!"

"It's an amazing plan!" said the short goblin with a smile.

"You're a genius," said the second goblin, bowing.

But the third goblin didn't say anything at all—he was too busy nibbling on a cupcake. Jack Frost saw him, gave a furious yell, and grabbed him by the ear.

"Listen to me, gargoyle face," he shouted. "If anyone's going to eat these cupcakes, it's going to be ME!"

With a bolt of icy-blue magic, he zapped the cake away from the goblin and shoved it into his own mouth.

"Now, you listen to me!" he shouted, spraying bits of cake all over the cowering goblins. "Find me lots and lots of cupcakes and bring them back to the Candy Castle— OR ELSE! I have a lot to do, so I have to get going!"

He pulled out a piece of paper and waved it under the goblins' noses. The girls leaned forward and saw, in messy handwriting:

Candy Castle—To Do List

Jack Frost reached
inside his cape and
pulled out something
that glimmered
under the lights. It
was small and
golden—and
shaped like a cupcake.
Coco gasped and grabbed Rachel's and
Kirsty's arms.

"Girls, that's my cupcake charm!" she
whispered.

Jack Frost handed the charm to the
short goblin, who had been making faces
at the girls earlier. He held it in both
hands, his eyes very wide.

"Thank you for trusting me with this,
boss," he babbled. "I promise that—"

"Enough!" Jack Frost snapped. "I don't have time to listen to you. Just hurry and bring me lots of beautiful cupcakes—or you'll all be sorry!"

Before the goblins could say another word, he disappeared with a rumble of thunder and a flash of icy magic.

Two of the goblins immediately turned to the cupcakes and started gobbling them down, but the short goblin put his hands on his hips.

"You shouldn't do that," he said. "Jack Frost wouldn't like it at all."

"Oh, you're such a goody-two-shoes!" sneered the first goblin.

The short goblin tried to grab the cupcakes back. When he did, all three of them started to wrestle.

"We have to get that cupcake charm back!" Rachel whispered to Kirsty and Coco. "Listen, while the goblins are fighting, maybe we could sneak up on them?"

"Let's try it," agreed Coco. "It's dangerous, but I can't stand to see my cupcake charm in that goblin's hand any longer!"

Icing to the Rescue

The three fairies tiptoed out from behind the cupcakes as quietly as they could and fluttered down to the middle tier of the cake stand.

"So far, so good," Kirsty whispered. "The goblins are too busy arguing to notice us."

They flew down to the bottom tier.
Still, none of the goblins noticed them.

"Now for the tricky
part," said Rachel.

She led the way
across the
bakery until
they were
hovering inches
behind the
short
goblin's
hand.
He clutched Coco's magic cupcake
charm tightly, but his attention was on
the other goblins. Rachel reached out
toward the charm . . .

Suddenly, the first goblin spotted her!
"Fairies!" he yelled.

"Where?" shouted the short goblin.

"Hide!" cried Coco.

The short goblin
spun around and
bumped into a
display table.
Cupcakes
tumbled
everywhere.

"Pick them up!"
he squawked.
"We can't damage
a single one!"

By the time the goblins
had picked up the cupcakes, each fairy
had landed on top of a cupcake and
posed like a candy decoration. Rachel,
Kirsty, and Coco stood as still as they
could while the goblins hunted all

around the shop
for them.
They looked
behind displays
and peered up
at the ceiling,
but couldn't find
the fairies anywhere.

"They must have left," the first goblin
said eventually. "All this searching has
made me hungry, though."

He turned to the display table and
picked up the cupcake that Rachel was
perched on. His mouth opened wide, and
Rachel gave a tiny gasp of fear. He was
about to eat her!

"Quick, Coco!" exclaimed Kirsty,
rising into the air. "We have to save
Rachel!"

As they zoomed upward, Rachel
darted away from the goblin's mouth,
holding her nose
so she couldn't
smell his bad
breath. The
goblin screeched
and swatted at
her as if she were
a fly.

"There they are!"
he squawked. "Get them! Stop them!"

Rachel, Kirsty, and Coco zigzagged as
fast their wings could carry them,
dodging the furious goblins. Bakery
boxes flew into the air and cake stands
crashed to the floor as the goblins ran
through the shop. But the short goblin
still had the magic charm in his hand,

and the fairies were getting tired. They
had to think of something fast!

Suddenly, Kirsty had an idea.

"Rachel, remember how I slipped on that icing earlier?" she panted. "If Coco can cover the floor in icing, that might stop the goblins."

As quick as a flash, Coco waved her wand. Instantly, the floor of Cupcake Corner was covered with a thick layer of gooey icing. The goblins slipped and slid across it, waving their arms to try and catch their balance.

"They look like three bad ice-skaters!" said Kirsty with a giggle.

"HELP!" squealed the short goblin, as his feet slipped in opposite directions.

With a *plop*, he landed on his bottom in the icing. The magic cupcake charm flew into the air, and Rachel dove toward it.

"Stop her!" howled the goblin.

The other two goblins leaped toward the charm, but they bumped their heads together and crashed to the floor, groaning. Rachel caught the beautiful charm and handed it to Coco. At once, it shrank to fairy-size! All three fairies breathed a big sigh of relief.

Coco waved her wand, and the icing on the floor disappeared. The cupcake stands and boxes were cleaned up in the blink of an eye. The goblins angrily scrambled to their feet.

"Give that back!" the short goblin demanded.

"Absolutely not," said Coco calmly. "It belongs to me."

"You should stop being so greedy," Rachel declared.

"And tell Jack Frost to stop being greedy, too," added Kirsty.

The first goblin clapped his hand over

his mouth with a horrified expression.

"What are we going to do about Jack Frost's cupcake throne?" He groaned. "Without the charm, we'll never find enough cupcakes for him!"

The Great Cupcake Sale

Coco gave Rachel and Kirsty a wink, and then waved her wand. A small cupcake with a tiny throne on top floated through the air toward the goblins.

"Jack Frost's never going to fit on that!" exclaimed the short goblin.

"It'll have to do," grumbled the second goblin.

He grabbed the cupcake and they all scurried out of the shop, arguing about who should be allowed to carry it.

"It's time for us to become human again, I think," said Rachel.

The three friends fluttered down behind the counter, and Coco turned the girls back to their normal size.

"I'm so grateful for your help, girls," she said, her eyes shining with happiness. "Now that I have my charm back, I know that cupcakes everywhere will be perfect again."

"We loved helping you," said Kirsty with a beaming smile. "Please tell the other Sugar and Spice Fairies that we're always here if they need us."

Coco blew them each a kiss, then twirled around and disappeared in a flurry of sparkling fairy dust. At that moment, the baker came out of the kitchen.

"Your cupcakes are all ready, sir—" he began, stopping when he saw that Jack Frost wasn't there anymore.

"I . . . um . . . I think he's gone," said Rachel.

"But I just made two hundred cupcakes for him!" the baker groaned. "What a waste! I'll never sell all of them this afternoon—it's almost closing time. At least I haven't put his picture on all of them yet."

He looked really upset, and the girls felt sorry for him.

"I have an idea," said Rachel. "How about having a special cupcake sale out on the street? Everyone will be on their way home from work. We'll help, if you'd like."

The baker smiled. "That's a wonderful idea," he said. "Thank you, girls! You can bring the cupcakes outside  once I set up the table."

Half an hour later, there was a huge crowd of people outside Cupcake Corner. Rachel and Kirsty couldn't fill the cake boxes fast enough! Everyone stopped at the cupcake sale on their way home from work, and most of them bought a box of cupcakes to take home as a treat.

"This blue frosting is so yummy!" said

a gray-haired man, filling his briefcase with cupcakes.

"My family will love these for dessert tonight," said a window cleaner, popping two cupcakes into her bucket.

By closing time, all of the beautifully decorated cupcakes had sold out.

"I'm sorry, girls, there isn't a single blue cupcake left for you to take home," said the baker. "But there will always be free cupcakes for you at Cupcake Corner. Thanks so much for your help!"

"Thank you!" exclaimed Kirsty. "That was fun!"

As they walked back to Kirsty's house, the girls talked about the day's adventures.

"I can't believe how much has happened today," said Kirsty. "We helped *three* fairies find their charms!"

"Yes, and we had yummy lollipops and delicious ice

cream," Rachel remembered, licking her lips. "It's too bad that we won't have any cupcakes tonight, though."

They reached Kirsty's house and went inside. In the kitchen, their cupcakes were still cooling. But they looked very different from before. . . .

"These cupcakes are perfect!" Kirsty said with a gasp. "I don't understand it— I thought we'd ruined them!"

"I think Coco must have stopped here on her way back to Fairyland," said

Rachel with a little smile. "Look."

She pointed to two of the cupcakes. The words *Thank you!* were written on them in sparkly gold icing. Rachel and Kirsty exchanged delighted grins.

"What beautiful cupcakes!" exclaimed Mrs. Tate, coming into the kitchen. "Cupcake Corner certainly does make perfect treats! Did you get those to thank Aunt Helen for the tickets to Candy Land?"

The girls glanced at each other, then nodded happily. They knew that Coco

had left the
cupcakes for
them, but they
didn't mind giving
them to Aunt
Helen. After all,
they weren't greedy
like Jack Frost and
his goblins!

"Are you looking forward to your tour
of Candy Land tomorrow?" asked Mrs.
Tate as she started getting dinner ready.

"Definitely!" said the girls together.

"We'll have to keep our eyes peeled for
Jack Frost and his goblins, though,"
Rachel whispered as they set the table.

"Yes, they still have four of the Sugar
and Spice Fairies' charms," Kirsty

agreed. "They're bound to be up to no good."

"And we're bound to be there to stop them," said Rachel with a laugh. "I can't wait for our next magical adventure!"

Rachel and Kirsty found Lisa, Esme, and Coco's
missing magic charms.
Now it's time for them to help

Clara

the Chocolate Fairy!

Join their next adventure in this
special sneak peek. . . .

Chocolate Crisis

"I'm so looking forward to this!" Rachel Walker told her best friend, Kirsty Tate, her voice brimming with excitement. The two girls were walking up one of the hills that overlooked Wetherbury. "I've never been to a candy factory before. I can't wait to see inside Candy Land."

"Me, neither," Kirsty agreed happily. "Wasn't it nice of Aunt Helen to arrange a tour of the factory for my birthday?" Kirsty's aunt worked in Candy Land's cookie department.

"Yes, and your birthday isn't until tomorrow, so it's almost like having an *extra* treat!" Rachel pointed out as they climbed higher up the hill. Ahead, they could see the factory and the big pink-and-white Candy Land sign over the wrought-iron gates. "Do you think we might get to try some treats while we're on the tour?" Rachel asked eagerly.

Kirsty grinned. "I hope so!" she replied. "I'm really looking forward to seeing the chocolate being made. My favorite kind is the Sticky Toffee Galore—it's a yummy toffee covered with chocolate!" Then Kirsty's smile faded. "Remember, though," she went on, "some of the treats might not taste very good, since Jack Frost and his goblins have the Sugar and Spice Fairies' magic charms."

Rachel nodded solemnly. Yesterday, right after she'd arrived to spend spring break with Kirsty, their old friend Honey the Candy Fairy had appeared to whisk the girls off to Fairyland. There they had met Honey's helpers—the seven Sugar and Spice Fairies! They looked after all the delicious, mouth-watering treats in Fairyland and the human world.

Rachel and Kirsty were very upset when they found out that Jack Frost and his goblins had stolen the Sugar and

Spice Fairies' magic charms. But they couldn't believe it when they found out *why* Jack Frost needed the charms—he'd ordered his goblins to build him a castle made entirely of candy and treats!

To make things worse, King Oberon and Queen Titania had explained to the girls that Treat Day was coming up very soon. On Treat Day, the king and queen gave each fairy in Fairyland a basket full of yummy treats to thank them for their hard work all year. But this year there wouldn't be any treat baskets at all if the magic charms weren't returned to the Sugar and Spice Fairies.

RAINBOW magic ™

Which Magical Fairies Have You Met?

- ❑ The Rainbow Fairies
- ❑ The Weather Fairies
- ❑ The Jewel Fairies
- ❑ The Pet Fairies
- ❑ The Dance Fairies
- ❑ The Music Fairies
- ❑ The Sports Fairies
- ❑ The Party Fairies
- ❑ The Ocean Fairies
- ❑ The Night Fairies
- ❑ The Magical Animal Fairies
- ❑ The Princess Fairies
- ❑ The Superstar Fairies
- ❑ The Fashion Fairies
- ❑ The Sugar & Spice Fairies

SCHOLASTIC

Find all of your favorite fairy friends at
scholastic.com/rainbowmagic

HIT entertainment

RMFAIRY9

RAINBOW magic™ SPECIAL EDITION

Which Magical Fairies Have You Met?

3 stories in each one!

- ❏ Joy the Summer Vacation Fairy
- ❏ Holly the Christmas Fairy
- ❏ Kylie the Carnival Fairy
- ❏ Stella the Star Fairy
- ❏ Shannon the Ocean Fairy
- ❏ Trixie the Halloween Fairy
- ❏ Gabriella the Snow Kingdom Fairy
- ❏ Juliet the Valentine Fairy
- ❏ Mia the Bridesmaid Fairy
- ❏ Flora the Dress-Up Fairy
- ❏ Paige the Christmas Play Fairy
- ❏ Emma the Easter Fairy
- ❏ Cara the Camp Fairy
- ❏ Destiny the Rock Star Fairy
- ❏ Belle the Birthday Fairy
- ❏ Olympia the Games Fairy
- ❏ Selena the Sleepover Fairy
- ❏ Cheryl the Christmas Tree Fairy
- ❏ Florence the Friendship Fairy
- ❏ Lindsay the Luck Fairy
- ❏ Brianna the Tooth Fairy
- ❏ Autumn the Falling Leaves Fairy
- ❏ Keira the Movie Star Fairy
- ❏ Addison the April Fool's Day Fairy

📖 **SCHOLASTIC**

Find all of your favorite fairy friends at
scholastic.com/rainbowmagic

HIT entertainment

RMSPECIAL12